The Case Of The

GREAT ELEPHANT ESCAPE™

Look for more great books in

series:

The Case Of The Summer Camp Caper™
The Case Of The Surfing Secret™

The Case Of The
GREAT ELEPHANT ESCAPE™

by June Doolittle

HarperEntertainment
A Division of HarperCollinsPublishers

A PARACHUTE PRESS BOOK

PARACHUTE PRESS

Parachute Publishing, L.L.C.
156 Fifth Avenue
New York, NY 10010

DUALSTAR PUBLICATIONS

Dualstar Publications
c/o Thorne and Company
A Professional Law Corporation
1801 Century Park East
Los Angeles, CA 90067

▉HarperEntertainment

An Imprint of HarperCollins*Publishers*
10 East 53rd Street, New York, NY 10022–5299

ISBN 0-06-106583-8

HarperCollins®, ▉®, and HarperEntertainment™ are trademarks of
HarperCollins Publishers Inc.

First printing: April 1999

Printed in the United States of America

Visit HarperEntertainment on the World Wide Web at
http://www.harpercollins.com

10 9 8 7 6 5 4

THE CIRCUS IS IN TOWN!

"**G**uess what?" I cried. "We have tickets for the Bixby and Burns Circus!"

Ashley, my twin sister, looked up from the computer. "Great, Mary-Kate," she said. "When?"

She didn't sound very excited. But that was because she was concentrating on her e-mail. Ashley loves to concentrate.

Everyone thinks that because Ashley and I look alike, we *are* alike. We're the same height. And we both have blue eyes and strawberry-blond hair. But Ashley is usually calm and logical. I get excited about almost everything.

"The tickets are for opening night!" I said. "That's tomorrow! Isn't that totally cool? You know, I've always wanted to join the circus."

Ashley grinned. "As a clown, maybe?"

"Ha-ha," I said. But I smiled back. Ashley and I love to tease each other.

"Who sent the tickets?" Ashley asked.

"Great-grandma Olive," I answered.

"She's the coolest!" Ashley declared.

Great-grandma Olive is our favorite relative. She's a detective! When we were little, she used to tell us all about the mysteries she solved. Soon we were hooked—we wanted to solve mysteries of our own.

So Great-grandma Olive told us to start our own detective agency. And we did! It's called the Olsen and Olsen Mystery Agency. Our attic is our headquarters. That's where

Ashley and I were talking.

"Ashley," I said, "you haven't heard the rest of my news. We're going to the Moonlight Circus Parade tonight!"

"What's that?" Ashley asked.

"It's what some circuses do when they arrive in a new place. All the performers march through town in a big parade."

Ashley's eyes lit up. "Animals, too?"

"Of course! The parade starts"—I looked at my watch—"oops, five minutes ago!"

"Then what are we waiting for?" Ashley logged off the computer and jumped up. "Let's go!"

We hopped on our bikes. We pedaled as fast as we could.

The parade was just entering the park when we caught up with it. Circus animals and performers gathered on the baseball diamond. Torches flickered in the dark. Shadows danced around the swirling crowd. Jugglers juggled and acrobats tumbled. In the center of the diamond a tiger roared!

"I'm glad he's in a cage!" Ashley told me.

All I could say was, "Wow!"

"It looks like the whole neighborhood is here," Ashley said.

Wheeling our bikes, we waded into the crowd. *Klonk!* I bumped into something— a huge hand.

I looked up. My eyes popped open wide. I was standing next to the fattest, tallest man I'd ever seen. The top of my head only came up to his hip! He wore a striped suit and a red top hat. His hat made him look even taller.

The giant laughed a deep, belly laugh. Then he said, "Hello there, little one. Don't be afraid. I'm Clyde Big, the World's Biggest Man."

Clyde stepped back. He covered his huge nose with his huge hand. "Achoo!" he sneezed. Then he said, "Excuse me!"

"Bless you," said Ashley.

Clyde took off his hat and bowed to Ashley and me. Then he gave us each a lollipop.

We thanked him and walked a little further. Suddenly Ashley pointed. "Look!" she cried. "A baby elephant!"

The baby elephant was so cute! She wore a purple coat with sequins and shells all over it. A purple hat sat between her huge, floppy ears.

A girl stood beside the baby elephant. She looked about ten years old—our age. She was dressed in purple, just like the elephant. Her leotard and skirt were covered in sequins and shells. Dozens of little shells were braided into her black hair. A gold elephant charm hung from a velvet ribbon around her neck.

"What a cute elephant!" I told the girl.

"Thanks!" the girl replied. "Her name is Baby Maysie. I'm Lakeisha." She petted the elephant's forehead. The elephant touched her cheek with the tip of its trunk.

"Is she yours?" Ashley asked.

"I take care of her. My family and I are elephant trainers," Lakeisha answered. "Tomorrow is our first show with the Bixby and Burns Circus. And it's Maysie's first show ever. I ride her and we do tricks together."

I petted Maysie's long, gray trunk. It was fuzzy!

"How do you go to school if you're in the circus?" Ashley wanted to know. "I mean, aren't you traveling all the time?"

"Yes," Lakeisha said. "But there are lots of kids in the circus, so we travel with our own teachers. One of the circus trailers is a schoolhouse."

"That sounds so cool!" I said. "I wish I could see it."

Lakeisha smiled. "I'd love to give you a tour—but not until after the opening. My family and I are pretty nervous about this new show."

"A tour would be terrific," I replied. "And I'm sure *you're* going to be terrific, too. We'll be in the audience tomorrow night!"

"Great. Why don't you give me your phone number?" Lakeisha said. "I'll call you about the tour."

Ashley handed her one of our Mystery Agency cards.

Lakeisha read it. Her eyes widened. "You two are the Trenchcoat Twins? Wow! You guys are famous! I've read about your mystery agency on *Kidz Online*."

"That's us," I said proudly.

Ashley looked at her watch. "Oops!" she said. "It's almost nine o'clock. We promised our mom we'd be home by then."

"Bye for now," I told Lakeisha. "And good luck tomorrow. We can't wait to see the show!"

We hopped back on our bikes. Lakeisha

waved. And so did Maysie, with her trunk!

The next morning after breakfast, I checked Olsen and Olsen's e-mail.

"Dee-duh-duh-dee!" sang the computer. That meant there was a message in our in-box. It was from Lakeisha. It read:

> Help! Maysie kidnapped! Come quickly!

"Ashley you've got to see this!" I called down the stairs. "Hurry!"

Ashley came running. She only had one shoe on. A hair clip hung from her mouth. She carried her other shoe in her hand.

"Look! Maysie's been elephant-napped!" I cried, pointing at the message on the computer monitor.

Ashley read it over my shoulder. "This is a case for Olsen and Olsen," she said.

"Definitely," I said. "We've got to help Lakeisha!"

I tried to slap Ashley five, but instead I slapped her shoe. We giggled. Ashley put down her shoe and we tried again.

While Ashley finished dressing, I wrote back to Lakeisha.

> Don't panic! We're on the case.
> We'll meet you underneath the
> circus banner in 30 minutes.
> Bring any clues.

I clicked SEND. Then I turned to Ashley. "It looks like we won't be going to the circus tonight after all."

"Right," Ashley said. "We're going right this minute!"

2

BUT HOW CAN YOU HIDE AN ELEPHANT?

We raced out to our bikes. Ashley scooped Clue into her bike basket. Clue is our pet basset hound. She's also the silent partner in our detective agency. I call her the Super-duper Snooper, because Clue has the best nose in the business.

"Achoo!" Clue sneezed. That morning she also seemed to have the biggest *cold* in the business.

We pedaled quickly through town to the big-top tent.

The circus banner flapped in the breeze. It was so big that we could read the words long before we got there.

We could also see someone pacing in front of the tent.

"That's Lakeisha," I said to Ashley. "She looks worried."

We reached the tent and parked our bikes. I lifted Clue out of the basket and set her down in front of the big-top tent.

"Achoo, ACHOO!" sneezed Clue.

"Bless you, doggie," said Lakeisha.

"Meet Clue," I said. "She has a cold."

"It's going around. Clyde Big is sick, too," said Lakeisha. She knelt and patted Clue's head. "Hello, Clue."

Then she looked up at me and Ashley. "Thanks for coming. We've got to find Maysie—and fast! I didn't tell anyone else she's missing. I don't want my family to worry. But she's the star of our act. If we don't find her by show time, 'The Travis

Family and Elephants' will be a flop!"

"Don't worry," Ashley said. "Olsen and Olsen are on the case."

"And Clue," I added. "Okay, let's get to work. When did you find out Maysie was gone?"

"This morning when I went to feed her," Lakeisha explained. "She wasn't in her stall! All I found was this note." She pulled a piece of paper from the pocket of her jeans. Her voice trembled. "It's from the kidnapper."

She handed the note to Ashley. The message on it was a computer printout. Too bad! Handwriting can be a clue—you can get writing samples from your suspects and see if any of them match up.

Ashley took the note and read it out loud. "'There'll be one less baby in the circus now!' That's weird," she said, frowning. "What do you think it means?"

"I don't know!" Lakeisha wailed.

"Hmmm," I said. "Well, maybe we should start by trying to find Maysie. Clue is really good at sniffing out missing animals. Once she found two hundred and two missing basset hounds!"

"Wow!" Lakeisha said.

I put the elephant-napper's note in my backpack.

"Do you have anything with Maysie's scent on it for Clue to sniff?" Ashley asked.

"Sure," Lakeisha answered. "Let's go to our trailer."

She led us to a fenced area behind the big-top tent. It was filled with brightly painted trailers. "All the members of the circus live in trailers," Lakeisha explained. "When they're all parked together, we call it the circus city."

A lady in a pink leotard walked out of the first trailer. She put a big, sparkly plastic jug on the ground, and waved at Lakeisha.

Then she squeezed herself into the jug!

Ashley's jaw dropped. "How did she do that? *I* would have a hard time fitting into that jug. And she must be twice my size!"

"That's Melba, the contortionist," Lakeisha explained.

"What's a contortionist?" I asked.

Lakeisha grinned. "It's someone who can bend her arms and legs in ways you can't even imagine!"

Melba popped out of the jug and winked at Lakeisha. "Can't wait to see Maysie on her big night. Good luck!"

Lakeisha smiled—but her eyes were worried.

"Now, let's be logical," Ashley said. "Maysie might be a baby, but she's still an elephant. How could anyone hide an animal that big?"

"Maybe she wandered off," I suggested.

Lakeisha pointed to the fence. It circled both the big top and the circus city. "She couldn't. That fence goes all the way around, and there are security guards, too. After dark no one is allowed in except members of the circus."

"So no one could have left with her," I said. "That means she must be here — somewhere!"

"It also means whoever took Maysie must be part of the circus," Ashley said.

Lakeisha gasped. "I can't believe anyone in the circus would steal Maysie!"

"I hope not," Ashley said. "But we can't rule anyone out yet. We'll have to question all the circus members."

"Let's say we're writing a story for our school newspaper," I put in. "That way no one will think it's weird when we ask them a bunch of questions."

"Good idea!" Ashley said, nodding.

We walked past a man in overalls. He set six torches in the ground. Then he lit them all. A sign on his trailer read: JERROLD THE

JUGGLER. One by one, Jerrold began to juggle the flaming torches. They whirled above him in a circle.

I stopped and stared. "Whoa!" I said. "That's amazing!"

"Lakeisha," Ashley said, "can you think of anybody in the circus who might *want* Maysie to disappear?"

"No way! Everyone loves Maysie," Lakeisha answered. "She's so cute and good-natured. I just can't imagine why anyone would want her gone."

We reached Lakeisha's trailer. Two huge smiling elephants were painted on its front.

"Remember, you guys, please don't tell my parents about Maysie," Lakeisha whispered to us. "They're already so nervous about tonight." She hung her head. "And I don't want them to know that I lost her."

"You didn't *lose* her," said Ashley. "Someone took her."

"But don't worry," I added. I zipped my

fingers across my mouth. "Our lips are sealed."

"Anyway," Ashley said, "we promise we'll find Maysie before your parents even know she's missing."

"And by show time, right?" Lakeisha asked.

I reached down and petted Clue. "Not a problem—especially with Clue on the job," I said. "She's got the best nose in the detective business!"

"Achoo!" said Clue.

At least—I hope *she does!* I thought.

3

CLUE LEADS THE WAY

We stepped into the Travises' trailer. It was really homey, with lots of braided rugs on the floor. On one end was a kitchen with a built-in dining table.

Lakeisha glanced out the back window.

"The coast is clear," she told us. "My parents are giving the elephants their baths."

I looked out the window. Mr. Travis stood on a ladder. He held a hose in one hand. A big elephant stood beneath it. Mrs. Travis was rubbing on elephant shampoo.

Two other elephants waited for their turn.

"They're so gigantic!" I said. "Even their footprints are huge!" I pointed to the big, round prints in the muddy ground.

Ashley laughed. "They look like prints from dinner plates!"

"Maysie's costumes are in my room," Lakeisha told us. She led us into a neat bedroom. A desk with a computer stood against one wall. Opposite the desk were a wardrobe and bunk beds.

Two piles of costumes sat on the desk. One pile was purple. The other was white and gold.

"Those purple costumes are the ones you and Maysie wore last night, right?" Ashley asked.

"Right." Lakeisha pulled a big baby bonnet from the white pile. "Maysie wears this in our Rock-a-Bye Baby number," she explained. "Maysie rides in a giant baby carriage. It's funny!"

Lakeisha gave me the bonnet. I stashed it in my backpack. *I'll give it to Clue to sniff when we're outside*, I thought.

I looked around the main room of the trailer. It had couches, a coffee table, and a TV. Circus posters hung on the walls. They all showed a little girl riding a huge elephant. They all read: THE TRAVIS FAMILY AND ELEPHANTS, FEATURING KALA!

"Who's Kala?" I asked. Then the front door banged open—and the girl from the poster walked in.

"*That's* Kala," Lakeisha said. "My little sister."

Kala looked just like Lakeisha—only smaller!

"Mom and Dad are out back," Lakeisha told her sister. "You'd better iron the elephant costumes. You were supposed to do that hours ago. I already did Maysie's."

"Oh, all right," Kala grumbled. She twisted the black velvet ribbon around her neck with her forefinger.

Lakeisha frowned. "Kala, where's your gold elephant charm?" she asked.

"I-I lost it, I guess," Kala stammered.

"Oh, no! We always wear those charms on opening night! You'd better find it," said Lakeisha. "Hurry, go iron the costumes. Then I'll help you look for the charm."

Kala made a face. "I don't need your help! I can find it myself," she snapped. Then she disappeared into the bedroom.

"I don't know what's the matter with Kala," Lakeisha whispered to us. "She's been so grouchy lately. And now she's lost her charm. No wonder everything is going wrong!"

"What do you mean?" I asked.

"My dad gave those charms to me, my mom, and Kala on the day Maysie was born," Lakeisha explained. "He said, 'Here's to celebrate a new baby in the family.' We've always had good luck since then. My

whole family is superstitious about it."
Lakeisha bit her lip. "What if Maysie got
kidnapped because Kala lost her charm?
Maybe that's bringing us bad luck!"

Ashley shook her head. "That's not logical," she said.

Lakeisha blinked back tears. "Maybe
not. But I believe it. I have to help Kala find
that charm." She sounded scared. "Before
something else terrible happens."

"We understand," I said. "You look for
the charm. We'll look for Maysie."

Ashley and I left the trailer. I pulled
Maysie's bonnet out of my pack. I held it to
Clue's nose. She took a big sniff.

"Woof-woof—ACHOO!" Clue said. Then
she took off!

Even with her cold, Clue was on the
scent! She pulled so hard that I lost the grip
on her leash. It went flying off behind her.
Fwap! Fwap! It slapped on the ground.

"Go, Clue!" Ashley shouted.

Thump! Thump! Thump! My heart started pounding as we raced after Clue.

We zigzagged through the trailers. All of a sudden Clue headed toward a trailer that was painted with huge orange and green polka dots.

A clown stood in front of the trailer. He bent down to tie his giant polka-dotted clown shoes.

Clue trotted up to the clown. "WOOF!" she barked.

The clown jumped—and lost his balance. He tumbled down and knocked over a huge bucket full of peanuts.

I clapped my hand to my forehead. "Whoops!"

The clown climbed to his feet and brushed himself off. "Who let you loose?" he grumbled to Clue. Then he caught sight of us. "Hey, is this your dog?"

"Yes, she is," Ashley said. "We're very sorry if she scared you."

The clown shook his head. "I'm having a bad week with animals! Last night that baby elephant sprayed my brand-new costume with mud. Now this basset hound attacks me. And me, just minding my own business!"

He shook his head and started picking up peanuts.

My eyes opened wide. "Ashley," I whispered, "this guy has a reason to be mad at Maysie. She messed up his new costume!"

"Right," Ashley whispered back. "I think we just found our first suspect!"

INSIDE CLOWN ALLEY

I grabbed Clue's leash. Ashley and I walked a little ways away from the clown. Then Ashley pulled out a pencil and her detective notebook.

The notebook was a gift from Great-grandma Olive. She says detectives should always takes notes on a case, so they won't forget anything important.

SUSPECT #1, Ashley wrote. CLOWN WITH POLKA-DOTTED SHOES. MOTIVE: MAYSIE RUINED HIS NEW COSTUME.

Motive is a word detectives use a lot. It means a suspect's reason for doing something.

I peered at the clown. He was trying to get all the peanuts back in the bucket.

Wait a second. Peanuts?

"He has to be the one who stole Maysie," I whispered to Ashley. "Look at all those peanuts! Elephants love to eat peanuts, don't they? Why else would the clown have a whole bucketful of them? He's hiding Maysie. And the peanuts are to keep her quiet!"

"That's logical," Ashley told me.

I grinned. Usually *she's* the logical one!

"Except for one problem," Ashley added. "How in the world could he hide an elephant in that trailer?"

I studied the clown's narrow trailer. I could see what Ashley meant. Maysie would never even fit through the door!

"Still, I think we should question him,"

Ashley said. "We can't rule him out."

We walked up to the clown. "Hi. My name is Mary-Kate, and this is my sister, Ashley," I began.

"Hello," the clown said. "I'm Marlon, the Head Clown."

"We're doing a story on the Bixby and Burns Circus for our school newspaper," Ashley said. "Could we interview you?"

"Sure!" Marlon agreed. "But you've got to come with me to Clown Alley. That's inside the big top. It's where we clowns put on our costumes and makeup."

Clown Alley! Wow! That sounded really cool.

We followed Marlon into the big top. Clown Alley was an area behind the arena. It was lined with dressing tables, trunks, and racks of costumes.

Marlon sat down at a dressing table and opened a big box. It was filled with makeup. He smoothed thick white greasepaint on his face. Then he patted his cheeks with powder.

He glanced at us in the mirror. "The Head Clown is the most important part of the circus! Put that in your newspaper."

Ashley began to write in her notebook.

"I heard that Baby Maysie the Elephant can do all sorts of wonderful tricks," I said. "And that she can even dance."

Marlon stroked red makeup around his mouth, nose, and chin. He pulled a tight, flesh-colored stocking cap down over his real hair. "Sure she can," he said. "But the elephant act isn't as good as the clown acts. The clowns are the *real* stars of the circus." He frowned. "Even though the posters make it look as if the elephants are the biggest deal."

Hmmm. He sounded jealous. That was suspicious!

Marlon pulled on an orange clown wig. He popped his clown nose onto his real nose. Then he picked up the bucket of peanuts.

"Uh—you must like peanuts, to have so many," Ashley said quickly.

"Well—" Marlon started to say.

Just then a shout came from the arena. "Marlon! It's time to practice the snakes-in-the-can gag."

"I've got to go," said Marlon. "Say, do you need any pictures for your article?" He pulled out a big photo of himself and signed it quickly. "Don't forget to write that I'm Head Clown," he told us.

Then he sprinted off.

Ashley let out a sigh. "Well, that wasn't very helpful. He left before we could find out anything from him!"

"I still say he took Maysie," I insisted. "He's jealous of the attention the elephants get! And don't forget the bucket of peanuts."

We stepped outside the big top. Clue started sniffing the air wildly.

"WOOF! WOOF! WOOF!" Clue began to jerk Ashley down the path on the leash. She pulled so hard the leash snapped!

"Clue!" we both yelled. "Come back!"

But Clue was running as fast as she could.

"She must smell Maysie!" I said. "Go, Clue! Lead us to her!"

We ran back through the circus city. Suddenly Clue skidded to a stop. She stood in front of a huge trailer. It must have been three times as big as the others.

In fact, *this* trailer was big enough to hold an elephant!

I looked at my sister. I could feel my eyes popping out.

"Ashley," I said, "I think we found Baby Maysie!"

5

THE SUPER-DUPER SNOOPER BLOOPER

Ashley pointed to a fancy sign on the door of the huge trailer. It read: HOME OF THE WORLD'S BIGGEST MAN — CLYDE BIG.

That explains the trailer's size, I thought.

"And look at this note," Ashley said. She pointed to a piece of paper that was taped on the trailer door. It read, "PLEASE do not disturb — I'm resting."

"There can't be an elephant *and* Clyde in there, too," I said, frowning. "The trailer isn't *that* big. Why would Clue take us *here*?"

Ashley sighed. "I think I know why." She scratched Clue behind her ear. "Clue's cold must be messing up her sense of smell," Ashley explained. "First she took us to Marlon the clown, and now Clyde Big. But there isn't an elephant in sight! She just can't sniff out Maysie. It's our Super-duper Snooper's first blooper!"

I petted Clue. "Poor dog," I said. "You probably have the same cold that Clyde Big has."

Clue whined and plopped down in front of Clyde's door.

"Still," I told Ashley, "we might as well check out the trailer, since we're here."

The blinds on the trailer were drawn, but one window was open. I climbed onto Ashley's shoulders, but I still couldn't reach the window. This trailer was so big, it made me feel tiny.

I hopped down off Ashley's shoulders.

"Just what we need!" said Ashley. She

pointed to a ladder attached to the side of the trailer. On its way to the roof it passed the open window.

I climbed up and leaned over. I pried open the blinds and peered in.

I saw an armchair that was as big as a bed, and a family-size dining table with only one chair. Clyde's trailer made Lakeisha's look like a dollhouse!

Then I saw a big mound on a gigantic bed. "Yep," I whispered to Ashley. "Someone huge is sleeping in there, under a flowered bedspread. And wearing a flowered nightcap!"

Ashley laughed. "For a big guy, that Clyde is pretty cute."

"WOOF! WOOF!"

"Clue's barking again," Ashley said.

"No kidding." I climbed down from the ladder. "I know you think her nose isn't working," I said, "but I say we should give her another chance. Let's go!"

Clue bounded off again. Ashley and I took off after her.

"Whoa!" I nearly crashed right into a man in a striped leotard and tights. He carried a paper bag in one hand.

"Aaaahh!" the man cried. He dropped his bag and leaped backwards—into a perfect back flip!

Ashley and I clapped. Then I picked up his bag and handed it to him. An apple and some grapes fell out onto the ground. Ashley picked them up.

"Thank you, young ladies," the man said with a grin. Then he hurried away.

Ashley and I looked at each other and giggled. The circus was such a fun place!

"WOOF! WOOF! WOOF!"

"That's Clue," Ashley said. "Come on, let's find her."

"She sounds excited," I said. "Maybe she found Maysie!"

We followed Clue's bark to a smaller tent

behind the big top. We poked our heads through the narrow opening flap.

I didn't see any elephants. Instead, the tent was full of fuzzy little dogs in frilly tutus!

Clue trotted over to us. Ashley grabbed her collar. "I take it back," she whispered. "Clue doesn't have a cold. She has the flu! She mixed up an elephant's scent with dogs'. Yikes!"

A big sign glittered on an easel beside the ring. It read: ZINA AND HER TERRIFIC TERRIERS. A thin, blond woman in high heels and a tight pink pantsuit stood in the center of the ring.

"That must be Zina," I said.

The terriers were doing all sorts of things that I never guessed dogs could do. They rode on skateboards, rolled on barrels, and climbed ladders. Zina held up a thin silver hoop. One by one, all the dogs leaped through it. Zina kept tossing out dog treats for rewards.

Finally, Zina sat down and clapped her hands. All the dogs stopped performing and jumped into her lap.

"Don't worry, pets!" Zina said, covering them with kisses. "I've taken care of every-thing. Tonight the world will see that *you* are the best animals in *this* circus!"

I poked Ashley with my elbow. "Did you hear that?" I whispered excitedly. "She said she's taken care of everything!"

"What do you think it means?" Ashley asked me.

"I'll tell you what it means to me," I said. I pulled out my mini tape recorder. Into the microphone I said, "We have our second suspect!"

ANOTHER FALSE ALARM?

"**W**hoa, Mary-Kate," Ashley said. "Don't jump to conclusions! Why do you think Zina is a suspect?"

"Because she wants to prove to the world that her dogs are the best animal act!" I explained. "She's jealous of the elephants. And she said she took care of everything. I think that means she took Maysie!"

Ashley frowned. After a minute, she nodded. "You could be right—but we don't have proof. We'd better talk to her," she whispered.

We tied Clue's torn leash to a tree. Then we stepped into the tent. "Excuse us," Ashley said politely.

Zina glanced up at us. "The show doesn't begin until tonight," she said. "I am rehearsing with my dogs now!"

"We're sorry to interrupt," I said. "It's just that—" I tried to think quickly. "We're such big fans."

"How sweet! You'd like my autograph," Zina cooed.

"Actually," Ashley said, "we'd like to interview you. We're writing a story about the Bixby and Burns Circus for our school newspaper."

"Lovely, lovely. But I cannot possibly speak with you now. I must rehearse. Come back after the show, darlings."

I had an idea. "We understand," I said quickly. "Is it all right if we look around and take notes now? We promise we won't bother you."

"Fine, darlings. Anything you like. Now, leave me, please!" Zina shooed us out of her small tent.

"Good thinking!" said Ashley when we were outside. "Now we can look for Maysie without making Zina suspicious!"

We looked around. A bunch of plastic dog cages were stacked in a pyramid. Next to the cages were tall crates for storing all the props.

Ashley poked me in the side. "There's room to hide an elephant behind all those cages and crates."

I grinned. Were we about to solve this mystery?

We carefully pushed one of the crates aside. I peered into the space behind the crates.

But there was no sign of Maysie—not even a peanut!

I shook my head. "I just don't get it," I complained. "How can we have so much trouble finding an *elephant*?"

"Hey, Mary-Kate! Ashley!" Lakeisha ran up. Her braids were flying. She was breathless. "There you are! I've been looking everywhere for you."

"Did you find the elephant charm?" Ashley asked.

"No," Lakeisha replied. "Kala is still hunting for it. I told her to take off her velvet ribbon. Then maybe Dad won't notice that the charm is missing." She gave us an anxious look. "Any sign of Maysie?"

"No," I told her. "But we do have some suspects. Like Zina. She wants to prove to the world that her terriers are a better act than your elephants." I sighed. "The problem is, we don't have any proof against Zina."

"There's also Marlon the clown," said Ashley. "We think he might have stolen

Maysie because he's jealous of all the attention the elephants get. Also, he was mad that Maysie sprayed his new costume with mud."

"But Maysie was just playing!" explained Lakeisha. "I can't believe Marlon is really mad. He loves Maysie!"

"Well, we *do* have some clues that point to him," Ashley said. "He had an entire bucketful of peanuts. He could be hiding Maysie and feeding her!"

"Good thinking," said Lakeisha. "Except the peanuts are for Marlon's act."

"Are you sure?" Ashley asked.

"Positive," Lakeisha answered. "Marlon pretends that he's an elephant and a trainer at the same time. He wears big floppy ears. Then he puts on a ringmaster's top hat and rewards *himself* with peanuts. Finally, he pretends to trip and knocks the bucket over. Peanuts fly all over the place. That skit always makes me laugh."

"Well, that gives Marlon a reason to have the peanuts," I said, "but he still could be sharing them with Maysie. After all, peanuts are an elephant's favorite snack!"

"That isn't really true," said Lakeisha, "Elephants don't like peanuts. In fact, most elephants won't eat peanuts at all. They prefer fruit—especially apples and grapes."

A lightbulb went off in my head. "Apples and grapes!" I cried. "That acrobat who I nearly ran into had a whole bag full of apples and grapes. Let's go!"

7

OUR FIRST REAL CLUE!

I clicked on my tape recorder. "We're on our way to interview suspect number three—the acrobat," I said. "He was carrying apples and grapes. He could be the one who's feeding Maysie. And *hiding* her. But we'll have to find him first."

"He was going that way," Ashley told Lakeisha. She pointed in the direction the acrobat went. "What's over there?"

"The costume tent," Lakeisha said. "That's probably where he went." She bit her lip. "I wish I could come with you to talk to him—but I have to go feed the elephants."

"That's okay, go ahead. We'll see you later!" Ashley said.

I glanced at my watch as Lakeisha hurried away. "But not *too* much later," I told Ashley. "The show starts in just a few hours. We've got to solve this case and find Maysie now!"

"Right. Let's go!" Ashley said. We grabbed Clue and ran to the costume tent. It was near the big top, not too far from Zina's tent.

We walked in and stared around. There were racks and racks of beautiful costumes. Some looked as light and fluttery as a butterfly's wings. Others were heavy costumes made of stuff that looked like metal. There was even a cape made of feathers!

A man stood at an ironing board, pressing the wrinkles out of a long banner. A woman sat near him, mending a costume.

I peeked around a clothing rack. There, standing in front of a full-length mirror, was the acrobat we saw earlier! He twisted his mustache and slicked back his wavy, jet-black hair. He turned this way and that, staring at himself.

Ashley took my arm. She pulled me over so the acrobat could see us in the mirror.

When he caught sight of us, he smiled. "Oh, hello," he said. "I am Otto the Great. You are the young ladies I saw before. I hear that you are friends of my dear LaKeisha, the girl from the elephant family." He frowned. "Oh dear. It is really me who is the elephant. My belly is getting so big!"

"Huh?" Ashley started to say. But I poked her with my elbow. I had just noticed something important!

"See!" I whispered. I pointed to a table. A large bowl full of apples and grapes sat on it.

Otto sucked in his stomach. "Do you think I am fat?"

I couldn't see an ounce of fat on his slim body.

"No way!" said Ashley. "We saw you do a back flip."

"You need to be in great shape to do that," I added.

"Oooof!" Otto patted his gut. "I've been eating too many hot dogs. They are so yummy! I love them!"

I pointed to the fruit. "It looks like you love apples and grapes, too."

"No, I don't," said Otto. "I hate them!"

Ashley and I looked at each other. Yes! We had our elephant snatcher!

Then Otto said, "The problem is, I love hot dogs. And popcorn. And cotton candy. And ice cream. This is all circus food and I am in the circus. But circus food makes me fat. And then I cannot perform my flips." He patted his stomach. "So today, apples and grapes are all that I am eating."

I sighed. So that was it! Otto had the apples and grapes to feed himself. Not to feed Maysie.

"WOOF! WOOF!" Clue barked from outside the costume tent.

"We'd better see if our dog is all right. See you later, Otto," I said. "You really do look great."

As Ashley and I left, I asked her, "Do you think Otto was telling the truth? He really isn't fat. And we can't just ignore all those apples and grapes, even if he says they're for his diet. I think we should keep him on our list of suspects."

"I agree," said Ashley. "But we have to keep searching for Maysie. We don't really have a main suspect. And it's almost show time."

"Arooo!" Clue threw her head back and howled. Then she put her nose to the ground again—and took off!

Ashley and I chased after Clue. She led us around the big top, past Zina's tent, past the entrance to Clown Alley.

"Where in the world is she going?" Ashley panted.

Clue zipped toward the circus city. Then she skidded to a stop. "WOOF! WOOF!" she barked, and started sniffing the ground like crazy.

I looked down—and gasped. In the dirt were round, flat footprints—elephant footprints. I remembered what they looked like from earlier in the day.

But these footprints were only half the size of the ones we saw earlier.

These were *baby* elephant footprints!

8

A TWISTED TRAIL

"**L**ook! Our first major clue!" I shouted. "Maysie the baby elephant was here—*right* here!"

The footprints made a path. We followed the path right to the door of a trailer. A sign on the door read OTTO THE GREAT.

I gasped. "Maysie went to Otto's trailer. He *is* guilty!"

"It sure looks that way," Ashley admitted. She frowned. "But I don't get it. Clue's nose hasn't been working right all day. How did she manage to follow Maysie's scent to these footprints? And another thing—how could Maysie be inside this trailer? It's no bigger than Marlon's trailer. It's way too small."

I studied Otto's door. My heart sank. Ashley was right!

I frowned, trying to figure it out.

"WOOF!" barked Clue. "ACHOO!"

Then she took off again!

We took off after her. "*Clue* sure doesn't seem to think Otto is guilty," panted Ashley. "She's taking us somewhere else."

We followed Clue around the corner—and found ourselves in front of Clyde Big's trailer!

Clue stood in front of the door, barking like crazy.

"Not again, Clue!" Ashley groaned. "We already checked this trailer once. Maysie isn't here!"

I put a hand over Clue's muzzle. "Calm

down, girl," I said. "You'll wake up poor Clyde."

Clue twisted away from me. "WOOF! WOOF!" she barked.

Then she flopped down on Clyde's doorstep.

"What is *wrong* with her?" asked Ashley.

"Maybe she has a fever," I suggested.

Ashley took a deep breath. "Let's go over what we know," she said. "First, Clue led us to Marlon the clown. Marlon has a motive—but there was no Maysie there."

"And it was the same when Clue led us to Zina," I said. "Zina has a motive, too—but Clue doesn't know that. Why did Clue lead us there? Zina didn't have the baby elephant."

Ashley made a note in her notebook. "And now, here we are back at Clyde Big's trailer," she said.

Suddenly an idea came to me. I snapped my fingers. "I've got it!" I said. "Maybe there's nothing wrong with Clue's nose at all. Maybe she's leading us all over the place because *Maysie* has been all over the place, too!"

Ashley's eyes lit up with excitement. "You mean whoever took Maysie is moving her around!"

"Exactly!" I said. "Maybe the thief has been having a hard time finding a good hiding place for an elephant."

Ashley grinned. "That isn't surprising!" she said. Then she clapped her hands together. "I just thought of something else. The thief could be sweeping away Maysie's footprints. That would explain why we only found them in that one spot. The thief must have just forgotten to sweep up once, by Otto's trailer."

I frowned. "But why did Clue bring us back to Clyde's trailer?" I wondered.

"Maybe the scent is strongest here," Ashley suggested.

"Ashley, I think we should go back over Clue's trail," I said. "We might have missed something."

We turned to go. I whistled to Clue. But she didn't budge.

"It seems like Clue wants to stay right here on Clyde Big's doorstep," Ashley said. "I guess she's tired."

I patted her. "Come on, Clue," I said.

Clue just stared at me with her big, droopy eyes.

"Okay," said Ashley. "She can stay here and rest if she wants. Let's retrace our steps. First stop is Marlon's trailer."

We rushed back to the polka-dotted trailer. The door was half open. We knocked.

No answer. We peeked in.

Even the furniture was orange-and-green polka-dotted! Other than that, though, there was nothing out of the ordinary.

"Next stop, Zina's," said Ashley. We jogged over to Zina's special practice tent and peeked inside. It was deserted, too.

"Look, Ashley!" I said. I pointed to a table. On it was a baby costume that looked a lot like Maysie's baby bonnet. And it was giant-size!

Ashley and I looked at each other. I could tell we were both thinking the same thing.

What is Zina doing with Maysie's costume?

We've got her, I thought. *Zina is the one!*

But before I could say a word, we heard Zina's voice outside the tent. "Come on, my pets!" she called. "Time to rehearse some more!"

Oh, no! What if Zina found us in here? We weren't ready to confront her yet. We needed to get all our facts straight first.

This could mean big trouble!

I grabbed Ashley's hand. We quickly ducked behind a cloth screen that stood in the corner.

A second later, we heard Zina and her dogs tromping into the tent. The dogs' collars jingled loudly.

Then I heard something terrible. Jingling. Growing louder.

One of the dogs was coming toward our hiding place!

Now I heard sniffing and snuffling. Then a brown-and-white terrier's head appeared around the edge of the screen. He looked at me and Ashley—and started to bark.

"What is it, pet?" Zina called. "What have you found?"

Footsteps came toward the screen. Then Zina's hand pulled the screen aside. She stared down her nose at Ashley and me.

Oh, no!

We were caught!

9

ONE HOUR TO DISASTER!

"What are you two doing here?" Zina demanded. "I told you—no interview until after the show."

"Uh—right," I said. I thought fast. "But Ashley dropped her lucky pencil somewhere. We came back to see if it was here."

Zina frowned. Did she believe us? I couldn't tell.

My heart was beating fast. I couldn't help glancing at Maysie's costume.

Zina saw where I was looking. She

snatched the costume off the table.

"Well, since you are here, perhaps you can do something for me," she said. "Will you be sweet and run this over to the Travises? And tell them I'm missing my terrier costumes. That costume delivery boy mixed things up again. He probably gave those elephant people the costumes for my darling dogs."

Zina put a hand on her hip. "Or maybe I should send this giant baby costume to Clyde Big," she said with a snicker. "That Clyde is such a baby. He has only a little flu—but he's gone home to Mama!"

I thought Zina sounded kind of mean. But I didn't say anything. I just wanted to get out of there!

Ashley took the huge baby suit. "We'd be glad to take the costume over to the Travises, Zina," she said.

"Thank you," said Zina. "Now—shoo, darlings. My pets and I must prepare ourselves for opening night. Out, out!"

Ashley and I picked up Clue from Clyde's doorstep, then hurried to Lakeisha's trailer.

"Do you think Zina was telling the truth about why she had Maysie's costume?" I asked. "I think she made it up. I think she stole Maysie!"

"Maybe," said Ashley. "But there's a simple way to find out. If the Travises have the dog costumes, then we'll know that Zina was telling the truth."

"You're right," I admitted. "Let's find out."

Nobody answered when we knocked on the Travises' door. "Maybe they're out back with the elephants," I said.

We ran around to the back of the trailer. Lakeisha's parents didn't notice us. They were working with three grown-up elephants. All of the elephants were dancing! Music played, and the big animals swayed and twirled. Mrs. Travis led the dance. She rode on a special elephant that wore a feathered headdress.

The elephant curtsied. Mrs. Travis slid down the elephant's trunk. The music played on. We could see that Mrs. Travis was asking her elephant to do something.

But the elephant just sank to the ground and closed her eyes!

Mrs. Travis looked worried. She walked over to her husband. Mr. Travis turned off the music.

"April refuses to do the twirl," said Mrs. Travis. "Nothing I can say or do will convince her. She's been like this all day. Something is bothering her."

"What can we do?" Mr. Travis asked.

"I guess we could keep April out of the show tonight," Mrs. Travis said. "But Maysie won't perform without her mother. And we can't keep Maysie out. She's the star!"

"Oh, boy," I whispered to Ashley. "Did you hear that? April is Maysie's mother. And if we don't find Maysie, April will mess up her own performance. Then the show won't go on at all."

We had to find Maysie. We *had* to!

I checked my watch again.

Uh-oh. We had only one more hour until show time!

THE ANSWER IS IN
THE...CHICKEN SOUP?

Mr. Travis spotted us. "Hello, girls," he called, and walked over. "Sorry, we didn't see you there. We're a little worried about April. She's not herself."

"You must be Lakeisha's friends, Mary-Kate and Ashley," said Mrs. Travis. She gave us a smile. "How's your newspaper story going?"

"Fine, thank you," I said.

"What do you have there?" asked Mr. Travis. He pointed to the bundle in Ashley's hand. "Is that Maysie's baby costume?"

"Yes," answered Ashley. "It was delivered to Zina by mistake. Did you get the dogs' costumes?"

"They're right here," Mr. Travis replied. He pointed to a small pile of costumes.

Ashley shot a glance at me. I knew what she was thinking. All our proof against Zina had just vanished!

Mrs. Travis turned to her husband. "Didn't you ask Kala to return those dog costumes an hour ago? She's been so careless lately. I wonder if I should have a talk with her."

"She's just being a seven-year-old," said Mr. Travis. "It's April we have to worry about. If she doesn't snap out of it by show time, we're in trouble."

"They have no idea how much trouble they're in *already*!" I whispered to Ashley.

"I have to check props in the big top," Mr. Travis said. "I'll drop Zina's costumes on the way. Would you girls find Lakeisha and give her Maysie's costume? I think she's been out searching for it."

"No problem," I said. "We're off!"

"Yikes," said Ashley when we were alone. "This is really serious. I bet the crowd is already beginning to take their seats in the big top. And we have no idea where Maysie is!"

"I know," I said gloomily. "It's ridiculous. What kind of detectives can't find a missing *elephant?*"

We went around the corner of the trailer and caught sight of Lakeisha and Kala a little ways off. Lakeisha was on her hands and knees searching through the grass. Kala was playing with a yo-yo.

Ashley frowned. "Kala's been trying to find her charm. That's why she wasn't at home doing her chores."

"But it seems as if Lakeisha is doing all the looking," I added. "Kala's just playing.

That doesn't seem fair, does it?"

Mrs. Travis came around the corner of the trailer. "Kala, there you are!" she called. "You should be in your costume by now! And your sister doesn't have time to play. She needs to get Maysie ready."

Scowling, Kala shoved her yo-yo into the pocket of her jeans. She walked back toward the trailer.

"Here, Lakeisha," said Ashley. She handed over Maysie's baby costume. "Your mom asked us to give you this."

Lakeisha's eyes darted back and forth between me and Ashley. "You didn't find Maysie, did you?" she asked.

"Not yet," I admitted. When I saw Lakeisha's eyes fill with tears, I felt terrible. "But we still have almost an hour!" I added quickly.

Lakeisha didn't answer. She just took the costume and trudged after Kala.

"Achoo!" sneezed Clue. "Achoo, ACHOO!"

Ashley patted Clue's head. "Clue really is sick," she said. "We should take her home and put her to bed."

"I wish we had time!" I scratched Clue's ear. "You need to go home and eat a big bowl of Mom's chicken soup," I told her.

And then I remembered something. Something very important.

"That's it!" I shrieked. "That's it! I know where to find Baby Maysie!"

11

BABY MAYSIE APPEARS

I grabbed Ashley's hand and started walking fast. Clue trotted along beside us. Now her tail was wagging.

"Clue might be sick," I said, "but she still has the best nose in the business. She was trying to tell us where Maysie was all along. We just didn't understand her!"

"I *still* don't understand," Ashley said. "Where are we going, Mary-Kate?"

"Clue wanted us to stay at Clyde Big's trailer," I explained. "And I know why."

"Why?" asked Ashley.

"Remember what Zina said about Clyde Big?" I asked Ashley. "She said: 'He has only a little flu and he's gone home to Mama!'"

Ashley stared at me. "So? Mary-Kate, I have no idea what you're talking about!"

"So do you think Clyde's mom lives in his trailer with him?" I asked. "I don't think so. I think Zina meant that Clyde went *home*, home—where his family is. He's not in his circus trailer."

Ashley's eyes lit up. "But *somebody* was there. Somebody was sleeping in the bed. Someone really big!"

Ashley and I gave each other a high five. Together we said, "Maysie!"

By this time we were in front of Clyde's trailer. Clue's tail was wagging a mile a minute. She sniffed eagerly at the door. She couldn't wait to get inside!

I turned the knob and pushed the door open. We went over to the bed. Gently I pulled back the bedspread.

And there she was—Baby Maysie! The little elephant was snoring softly. Clyde's flowered nightcap covered her floppy ears.

She'd been napping in Clyde's trailer all along!

"You were right, Mary-Kate," said Ashley. "Someone made us think Maysie was Clyde Big. But who did it? Marlon? Otto? Zina?"

Then I saw a small broom leaning against the wall. "Look! That's what the thief used to brush away Maysie's footprints."

"And look over there," said Ashley. "A pile of hay. And a bowl of water. Someone has been feeding Maysie."

I noticed something glinting in the hay. Something golden. "Ashley, check it out. What is that shiny thing?"

Ashley bent over. She plucked something tiny and golden out of the hay pile. We both stared at it.

"It's an elephant charm!" I exclaimed.

"It must be the one Kala lost," Ashley said. She frowned. "And that means…"

"It means Kala is the one who took Maysie!" I finished.

I couldn't believe it! *Kala* was the elephant thief?

We never even thought of her!

"Right," Ashley agreed. "Kala is the one who led Maysie all over the circus city. This was the hiding place she finally found."

"Pretty smart," I said. "Clyde and Maysie are the same size!" I shook my head. "But why, Ashley? Why did Kala do it?"

"That's the big question," Ashley said. She tucked the elephant charm into her pocket. "Let's find Kala—and ask her!"

THE BEST SURPRISE EVER!

First we had to wake Maysie. I sat down beside the baby elephant. She was still snoring. I rubbed her trunk gently.

Slowly Maysie opened her eyes. She pulled herself up and yawned. Then she stretched her trunk and flapped her ears.

"She's so cute!" Ashley said, laughing.

Ashley took Maysie's harness. We led her out of the trailer. Clue danced along beside us, yipping happily.

"Good job, girl!" I told her.

We spotted Kala and Lakeisha near their trailer. They were waving a metal detector over the ground! It looked like a strange vacuum cleaner. It made a high, whiny noise as it moved.

"They must still be looking for Kala's charm," I said.

The girls were so busy, they didn't even see us—or Maysie—until we were practically on top of them!

When Lakeisha saw Maysie her whole face lit up. She dropped the metal detector. *Klonk!* Then she ran over and hugged her baby elephant.

"Maysie, I'm so happy you're all right!" Lakeisha cried. She glanced at me and Ashley. "Thank you, thank you!"

Ashley held up Kala's charm. "Oh, you found Kala's charm too!" Lakeisha cried. "It must have brought you luck!"

"Sort of," Ashley said. She handed the charm to Kala.

"Where did you find Maysie?" Lakeisha asked.

Ashley and I both looked at Kala. She was staring down at the ground and shuffling her feet. She looked as if she wished she were anywhere else.

"We found Maysie in Clyde Big's trailer," I told Lakeisha.

"You mean Clyde took her?" Lakeisha's eyes widened. "I can't believe it! He seems so nice."

"Actually," said Ashley, "it wasn't Clyde who took her. Clyde has the flu. He went home to be with his family."

"Huh?" Lakeisha frowned. "So then who did take her?"

"Kala, maybe you should answer that," I said gently.

Kala burst into tears. "Oh, Lakeisha," she wailed. "*I* took Maysie. I'm so sorry!"

"*You* took Maysie?" Lakeisha looked shocked. "Why?" she asked. "Why in the world would you do that, Kala?"

"Because—because I was jealous," Kala mumbled. She sniffed and wiped tears from her cheeks. "Nobody pays any attention to me anymore. It's Maysie, Maysie, Maysie all the time!"

Ashley and I looked at each other. So that was it!

"I wasn't going to hide her forever. Just until opening night was over. I thought maybe if Maysie missed the first show, I'd get to be the star again," Kala explained. "Then everything would go back to the way it used to be."

"Now I understand what the elephant-napper's note meant," Ashley whispered to me. "Kala wanted to be the baby of the family again."

Lakeisha's mouth was open in surprise. After a minute, she said, "Wow, Kala. I didn't know you were feeling so bad!"

"How did you do it?" Ashley asked.

"After all, an elephant is pretty hard to hide!"

"That's what had us confused all day," I added.

Kala took a deep breath. "I had to do it while everyone was asleep. Very early this morning, I took Maysie from her stall. I took a broom with me to brush away her footprints. We walked all over the place. I was looking for a good place to hide her."

"You must have gone right past Marlon's trailer, and Otto's trailer," I said. "Our dog Clue led us there. But we couldn't figure out why."

Kala nodded. "At first I thought I could put her in Zina's tent—but Zina was already in there with her dogs. So I went back to see if I could find someplace else. Then I saw a note on the door of Clyde's trailer. It said he went home sick."

"And Clyde's trailer was the perfect size for an elephant," Ashley said.

"Right," Kala agreed. "So I put Maysie in the bed inside."

A small grin crept across Lakeisha's face. "Well, that was good thinking. Maysie really loves to sleep!" she said.

"Right," Kala went on. "I put up a 'Do Not Disturb' note, and swept up all of our footprints that I could find. After that I came back to our trailer and crawled back into my own bed. And nobody ever noticed I was gone." Kala gave her sister a pleading look. "Please don't be angry with me, Lakeisha."

"I'm not—I guess," Lakeisha said. "I mean, I am angry, but I sort of understand why you did it. And I'm sorry you've been feeling so terrible." She put her arm around Kala's shoulders. "But next time—don't steal an elephant. Just talk to me about it, okay?"

We all laughed. Then Kala's face grew serious again.

"I guess I'm in pretty big trouble," she said.

Lakeisha shook her head. "Don't worry. Mary-Kate and Ashley and I are the only ones who know Maysie's been missing. And we won't tell."

"Actually, someone else knows too," Ashley said.

Lakeisha and Kala looked horrifed. "Who?" they said at the same time.

I knew what Ashley meant. "April!" I answered. "Maysie's mom has been missing her baby."

"Poor April! Let's get them back together," said Lakeisha. "And quick, so we can all get into our costumes. We've got just enough time. And speaking of time, you'd better get to your seats, Mary-Kate and Ashley. The show will start soon."

Lakeisha hurried toward the trailer. But Kala hung back. She still looked sad and worried.

Lakeisha grabbed Kala's hand. "Come on. I know just how to cheer you up," she said.

"How?" asked Kala.

Lakeisha winked at her sister. "It's a secret!"

Ashley and I stopped at the snack stand and bought cotton candy and sodas. Then we went to find our seats. They were right in the very front row!

"This is going to be so great!" I said as we sat down.

The lights went dim. The crowd hushed.

And the circus music began!

The Travis Family and Elephants were the first ones in the opening march. Ashley and I cheered as the elephants paraded in. The jewels on their costumes flashed and glittered in the ring lights.

Ashley let out a gasp. "Look, Mary-Kate! Lakeisha isn't riding Maysie. Kala is!"

I couldn't help grinning. Kala and Baby Maysie led the parade! A spotlight followed every move they made.

"That must be the surprise Lakeisha was talking about," I said.

Lakeisha rode on April, Maysie's mother. And behind them were Mr. and Mrs. Travis on their elephants. Everyone, including the elephants, wore their fancy purple costumes, covered with sequins and shells. Tiny golden elephants twinkled from *both* of the girls' necks.

But it turned out I was wrong about the surprise. Kala riding Maysie was only half of it!

I couldn't believe my eyes when Kala and Lakeisha rode right up to our seats! Maysie and April knelt down. "Mary-Kate and Ashley, hop on!" Kala called. "You're the reason that *both* Maysie and I are here tonight. Thank you!"

"You're welcome!" I said. And Ashley

and I climbed onto the elephants!

I sat in front of Kala on Maysie. Ashley sat in front of Lakeisha on April. We waved from our elephants as we bobbed around the ring. Everyone in the audience clapped like crazy!

So I did join the circus after all—at least for a few minutes. And it was even more fun than I dreamed—because Olsen and Olsen had just cracked another case!

Hi from the both of us,

Ashley and I were off to summer camp! We were so excited. Horseback riding… swimming…arts and crafts…and no mysteries to solve. We were hanging up our trenchcoats for eight whole weeks!

Or were we?

The trouble started when one of our bunkmates accused me of stealing her cookies. Then another camper's candy turned up—in my pillowcase! I didn't take the cookies—or the candy. But Ashley and I had to discover who *did*—before I got kicked out of Camp Wishing Well!

Want to find out some more? Read on for a sneak peek at *The New Adventures of Mary-Kate & Ashley: The Case Of The Summer Camp Caper.*

See you next time!

Love,

Ashley Olsen + Mary-Kate Olsen

A sneak peek at our next mystery…

The Case Of The
Summer Camp Caper

Back at our bunk, Patty O'Leary climbed up on her bed. "I'd rather rest than write letters. All these sports are wearing me out!"

But after a few seconds, Patty started tossing and turning. "Oooh!" she muttered.

"What's the matter, Patty?" Amy, our camp counselor, asked.

"These camp pillows are as flat as pancakes," Patty said. "At home I have two big, fluffy pillows—with ruffles!"

"You can use my pillow, Patty," I said. "I don't need it to write letters."

I reached for my pillow. But as I handed it over to Patty something weird happened.

A shower of Gooey Chewy and lollipop wrappers fluttered out of my pillowcase!

"Hey!" I shouted, as the wrappers fell to the floor. "How did those get in there?"

Amy and my bunkmates stood around the heap of wrappers. There were a few un-wrapped candies as well.

"As if you didn't know!" Jackie said.

"What do you mean?" I asked.

Jody pointed to the wrappers. "Gooey Chewies...rainbow lollipops. You're a thief. *You* stole Angela's care package, Mary-Kate. It's totally obvious!"

"What's the matter, Mary-Kate?" Veronica sneered. "Weren't my cookies enough?"

"Why do you have to steal?" Patty asked me. "Can't your parents afford to send you your own candy?"

I wanted to speak, but my mouth felt incredibly dry. Luckily, Ashley said it for me.

"Mary-Kate would *never* steal anything," Ashley declared. "She doesn't even like Gooey Chewies. Right, Mary-Kate?"

I nodded. "They stick to my teeth!"

"Then how did the candy wrappers get into your pillowcase?" Amy asked me.

"I don't have a clue!" I cried.

Amy stared at the candy wrappers. Then she stared at me.

"This doesn't look good, Mary-Kate," she said.

"I know," I answered sadly.

Amy stared at me a moment longer. Then she shook her head. "All right, everyone, I'll talk to the other counselors and deal with this later," she said. "Why don't you all go back to what you were doing?"

The other girls returned to their beds. While they wrote letters, Ashley climbed up on my bed.

"I think you're being framed, Mary-Kate," she whispered. "Someone wants everybody to believe that you're stealing the goodies."

"But who?" I asked. "And why?"

Ashley leaned over. "That's what we have to find out!"

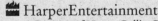

Don't Miss

Mary-Kate & Ashley

n their 2 newest videos!

Available Now Only on Video.

Listen To Us!

Ballet Party™

Birthday Party™

Sleepover Party™

**Mary-Kate & Ashley's Cassettes and CDs
Available Now Wherever Music is Sold**

It doesn't matter if you live around the corner...
or around the world....
If you are a fan of Mary-Kate and Ashley Olsen,
you should be a member of

Mary-Kate + Ashley's Fun Club™

Here's what you get
Our Funzine™
An autographed color photo
Two black and white individual photos
A full sized color poster
An official Fun Club™ membership card
A Fun Club™ School folder
Two special Fun Club™ surprises
Fun Club™ Collectible Catalog
Plus a Fun Club™ box to keep everything in.

To join Mary-Kate + Ashley's Fun Club™, fill out the form below
and send it along with

U.S. Residents	$17.00
Canadian Residents	$22.00 (US Funds only)
International Residents	$27.00 (US Funds only)

Mary-Kate + Ashley's Fun Club™
859 Hollywood Way, Suite 275
Burbank, CA 91505

Name:_____

Address:_____

City:_____ St:_____ Zip:_____

Phone: (_____) _____

E-Mail:_____

Check us out on the web at
www.marykateandashley.com